Geronimo Stilton
ENGLISH!

⑥ LET'S KEEP FIT! 一起來健身！

新雅文化事業有限公司
www.sunya.com.hk

Geronimo Stilton English
LET'S KEEP FIT!　一起來健身！

作　　者：Geronimo Stilton 謝利連摩・史提頓
譯　　者：申倩
責任編輯：王燕參
封面繪圖：Giuseppe Facciotto
插圖繪畫：Claudio Cernuschi, Andrea Denegri, Daria Cerchi
內文設計：Angela Ficarelli, Raffaella Picozzi
出　　版：新雅文化事業有限公司
　　　　　香港筲箕灣耀興道3號東匯廣場9樓
　　　　　營銷部電話：（852）2562 0161
　　　　　客戶服務部電話：（852）2976 6559
　　　　　傳真：（852）2597 4003
　　　　　網址：http://www.sunya.com.hk
　　　　　電郵：marketing@sunya.com.hk
發　　行：香港聯合書刊物流有限公司
　　　　　香港新界大埔汀麗路36號中華商務印刷大廈3字樓
　　　　　電話：（852）2150 2100　傳真：（852）2407 3062
　　　　　電郵：info@suplogistics.com.hk
印　　刷：C & C Offset Printing Co.,Ltd
　　　　　香港新界大埔汀麗路36號
版　　次：二〇一一年二月初版
　　　　　10 9 8 7 6 5 4 3 2 1

CONTENTS
目 錄

BENJAMIN'S CLASSMATES 班哲文的老師和同學們　4

GERONIMO AND HIS FRIENDS 謝利連摩和他的家鼠朋友們　5

LET'S GO TO THE GYM! 一起去健身室！　6

I LOVE EXERCISING 我愛做運動　8

A SONG FOR YOU! - I Love Exercising!

A FOOTBALL MATCH 足球比賽　10

A TENNIS MATCH 網球比賽　12

AT THE SWIMMING POOL 在游泳池　14

A BASKETBALL MATCH 籃球比賽　16

HOORAY FOR SPORTS! 運動萬歲！　18

A SONG FOR YOU! - I Love Sports!

A STINKY DRAW 發出惡臭的足球比賽 　20

TEST 小測驗　24

DICTIONARY 詞典 　25

GERONIMO'S ISLAND 老鼠島地圖　30

EXERCISE BOOK 練習冊

ANSWERS 答案

BENJAMIN'S CLASSMATES
班哲文的老師和同學們

Maestra Topitilla
托比蒂拉·德·托比莉斯

Rarin
拉琳

Diego
迪哥

Rupa
露芭

Tui
杜爾

David
大衛

Sakura
櫻花

Mohamed
穆哈麥德

Tian Kai
田凱

Oliver
奧利佛

Milenko
米蘭哥

Trippo
特里普

Carmen
卡敏

Atina
阿提娜

Esmeralda
愛絲梅拉達

Pandora
潘朵拉

Takeshi
北野

Kuti
菊花

Benjamin
班哲文

Hsing
阿星

Laura
羅拉

Kiku
奇哥

Antonia
安東妮婭

Liza
麗莎

GERONIMO AND HIS FRIENDS
謝利連摩和他的家鼠朋友們

謝利連摩·史提頓 Geronimo Stilton
一個古怪的傢伙,簡直可以說是一隻笨拙的文化鼠。他是《鼠民公報》的總裁,正花盡心思改變報紙業的歷史。

菲·史提頓 Tea Stilton
謝利連摩的妹妹,她是《鼠民公報》的特派記者,同時也是一個運動愛好者。

班哲文·史提頓 Benjamin Stilton
謝利連摩的小侄兒,常被叔叔稱作「我的小乳酪」,是一隻感情豐富的小老鼠。

潘朵拉·華之鼠 Pandora Woz
柏蒂·活力鼠的小侄女、班哲文最好的朋友,是一隻活潑開朗的小老鼠。

柏蒂·活力鼠 Patty Spring
美麗迷人的電視新聞工作者,致力於她熱愛的電視事業。

賴皮 Trappola
謝利連摩的表弟,非常喜歡食物,風趣幽默,是一隻饞嘴、愛開玩笑的老鼠,善於將歡樂傳遞給每一隻鼠。

麗萍姑媽 Zia Lippa
謝利連摩的姑媽,對鼠十分友善,又和藹可親,只想將最好的給身邊的鼠。

艾拿 Iena
謝利連摩的好朋友,充滿活力,熱愛各項運動,他希望能把對運動的熱誠傳給謝利連摩。

史奎克·愛管閒事鼠 Ficcanaso Squitt
謝利連摩的好朋友,是一個非常有頭腦的私家偵探,總是穿着一件黃色的乾濕樓。

LET'S GO TO THE GYM!
一起去健身室！

親愛的小朋友，我曾經答應過柏蒂小姐今年夏天要陪她去沙灘，但當我嘗試穿泳裝時⋯⋯我以一千塊莫澤雷勒乳酪發誓，我沒有像我妹妹菲那樣的健美體態，也沒有像我朋友艾拿那樣健壯的體型⋯⋯我不想當懶豬，因此我可愛的侄兒班哲文和潘朵拉提出陪我一起去健身室⋯⋯

跟我謝利連摩‧史提頓一起學英文，就像玩遊戲一樣簡單好玩！

你可以一邊看着圖畫一邊讀。
以下有幾個標誌，你要特別留意：

當看到 💿 標誌時，你可以聽CD，一邊聽，一邊跟着朗讀，還可以跟着一起唱歌。

當看到 ⭐ 標誌時，你可以和朋友們一起玩遊戲，或者嘗試回答問題。題目很簡單，它們對鞏固你所學過的內容很有幫助。

當看到 ❗ 標誌時，你要注意看一下格子裏的生字，反覆唸幾遍，掌握發音。

最後，不要忘記完成小測驗和練習冊裏的問題！看看你有多聰明吧。

祝大家學得開開心心！

謝利連摩‧史提頓

I LOVE EXERCISING
我愛做運動

一到健身室，我就碰到了老闆查高坦圖，他可真是個肌肉男啊！當我還在用驚歎的目光注視着老闆的時候，班哲文和潘朵拉已經開始和他們的朋友們一起玩了！

Good morning, Geronimo! Are you here for some exercise?

No, thanks... but the kids would love to.

parallel bars

Very well, let's start then!

vaulting horse

mattress

high jump crossbar

gym mat

> ❗ I would prefer the ribbon.
> 我比較喜歡玩彩帶。
>
> I would prefer jogging.
> 我比較喜歡跑步。

I would like to do some exercises with the ball.

I would prefer the ribbon.

balance beam

8

I Love Exercising!
I would like to train for the high jump,
I would like to exercise with a hoop or a ball,
I enjoy using the parallel bars,
I enjoy doing the splits.
and the cartwheel, I would like
to exercise with my friends,
I would like to exercise with you!

I would like to practice the high jump.

I would prefer jogging.

jump
跳

split
劈腿

pirouette
腳尖旋轉

cartwheel
側手翻

somersault
翻筋斗

push-ups
掌上壓

gymnastics
體操

climbing pole

rings

rope

A FOOTBALL MATCH
足球比賽

踢足球是一種很好的運動！有句名言說得好：一支訓練有素的隊伍可以讓整個世界着迷！讓我們一起來學習關於足球的英文詞彙吧！

football match

fans

stadium

flag

banner

referee   whistle

goalkeeper

goal

linesman

uniform

kick-off

football

football player

captain

football pitch

football team

GOAL

Benjamin has scored a goal.
His team is leading: 1-0!

FOUL

A player from the rival
team has fouled.

PENALTY KICK

The referee blows his whistle
for a penalty kick: Rarin has to
take the penalty kick.

SAVE

The goalkeeper makes a fine
save! Benjamin's team wins
the match 1-0.

I don't like playing
football.
我不喜歡踢足球。

*No, thank you.
I don't like playing
football.*

*Would you
like to play
football,
Uncle G?*

A TENNIS MATCH 網球比賽

我覺得足球並不太適合自己，於是班哲文和潘朵拉便帶我去看他們的朋友安東妮婭和田凱正在進行的網球比賽！

試着用英語說出以下句子：

(a) 我喜歡打網球。

(b) 我比較喜歡踢足球。

潘朵拉真細心呀，她很快就發現網球比賽中評判用的術語大部分是英文。她一邊看比賽，一邊問我那些英文詞彙是什麼意思，我便一一解釋給他們聽，例如「比賽」英文叫做「match」，每場比賽會分為「game 局」和「set 盤」。誰最先贏得 6 盤，誰就贏得該局。

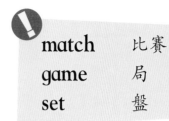

match	比賽
game	局
set	盤

Antonia is the first to serve.
Tian Kai replies with a very
strong forehand.

Antonia replies with a
backhand, Tian Kai replies
with a volley.

Antonia comes up to the net
and smashes.

You have been a formidable opponent.

results

you have been
你是

Antonia wins
the match!

13

AT THE SWIMMING POOL
在游泳池

也許我應該去游泳池，游泳是非常好的運動，它可以平衡地鍛煉全身肌肉！

swimming trainer

diving board

swimming lesson

starting block

swimming pool

bathing cap

lane

swimming goggles

swimming costume

changing room

shower

locker

hairdryer

bathrobe

flip-flops

towel

在游泳池裏，大家自由自在地游着，各自都有自己喜歡的泳式。
為了增加趣味，潘朵拉組織了一場水球比賽！

比賽十分激烈，孩子們都玩得很開心。

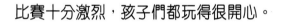

⭐ 試着用英文説出以下句子：
(a) 我喜歡自由泳。
(b) 我比較喜歡背泳。

❗ support 支持

答案：
(a) I like the crawl.
(b) I prefer the backstroke.

A BASKETBALL MATCH
籃球比賽

接着，班哲文和潘朵拉邀請我去看一場籃球比賽。雖然他們知道這不是適合我的運動，因為我的投球技術差極了，我連往自己辦公室的垃圾桶內投廢紙球也投不中！

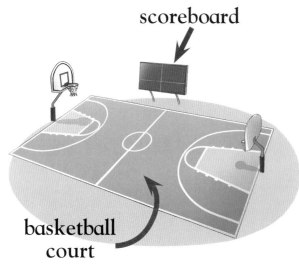

scoreboard

basketball court

to shoot hoops

basketball stand

7

extra time

time out

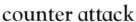

counter attack

vest

knee pads

referee

shorts

trainers

⭐ 試着用英語説出以下詞彙：運動短褲、運動背心、護膝、運動鞋。

Sakura dribbles very well.

Mohamed scores two points with a slam-dunk.

Excellent shot, Liza!

With two free throws, Milenko's team wins the match.

⭐ 穆哈麥德在做什麼？請用英語回答。

答案：Mohamed scores two points with a slam-dunk.

HOORAY FOR SPORTS!
運動萬歲！

　　班哲文和潘朵拉還向我推薦了很多其他運動。但我以一千塊莫澤雷勒乳酪發誓，惟一能引起我興趣的，只有馬克斯爺爺很多年前教過我的運動——高爾夫球！那麼你又喜歡哪項運動呢？一起來看看下面班哲文和潘朵拉的介紹吧！

1 Track and Field
athlete
100 meter race
hurdle race
shot-putting
long jump
high jump

2 Horse Riding
horse
rider

3 Martial Arts
judo
karate

4 Archery
bow
arrow
target

5 Cycling
cyclist
racing bicycle
mountain bike

6
roller-skating
rollerblades
ice-skating
ice skates
speed skating
figure-skating
ice hockey
field hockey

★ 試着用英語説出以下詞彙：跳高、跳遠。

7 Fencing

foil

8 Volleyball

volleyball player
net

9 Water Sports

windsurfing
sailing
canoeing

10 Golf

club
ball
hole
green

I used to
play golf with
Grandpa Torquato!

A SONG FOR YOU! Track 2

I Love Sports!

Yes, I know: I am a little lazy,
I don't like martial arts,
I hate archery,
but I like golf very much.

It's nice to do sports,
it makes you feel good.
If you go in for sports,
you'll grow up healthy and strong!

Yes, I know: I am a little lazy,
I don't like speed skating,
I hate shot-putting,
but I like golf very much.

It's nice to do sports,
it makes you feel good.
If you go in for sports,
you'll grow up healthy and strong!

跳高 : high jump, long jump

19

A STINKY DRAW

〈發出惡臭的足球比賽〉

旁述員：由鼠民公報和國家乳酪生產商舉行的足球友誼賽即將展開！

菲：這就是鼠民公報球隊的守門員謝利連摩·史提頓了。

謝利連摩：吁……單是跑出場，已經累死我了。

潘朵拉：加油呀，叔叔！
班哲文：我們現在領先三比零！
謝利連摩：對，但當他們的前鋒進攻到這裏來時，我就完蛋了。

艾拿：有我們兩個後衛……
查高坦圖：你不用擔心啦，謝利連摩！

謝利連摩：可，但……哇！
班哲文：謝利連摩叔叔被他們身上發出的乳酪氣味催眠了！

但是半小時之後……
查高坦圖：我已筋疲力盡了。
艾拿：我也是。
謝利連摩：小心啊，他們準備射球了！

旁述員：入球了！現在的得分是三比一。
班哲文：幸好比賽快結束了！

但是，不一會兒後……

潘朵拉：謝利連摩叔叔，他們又準備射球了！

旁述員：小心橫邊抽射……

旁述員：又入一球！三比二！

旁述員：真是令人難以置信啊！國家乳酪生產隊扭轉了局面。

旁述員：乳酪生產隊得到一個罰球！

潘朵拉：不不不！

旁述員：各位先生女士，這將是決定性的一球……

潘朵拉：我有辦法！

旁述員：大家留心……準備射球了……

旁述員：守門員成功救到球了！ 班哲文：叔叔，你好屬害啊！

謝利連摩：我現在可以把鼻子上的衣夾摘下來嗎？
潘朵拉：當然可以！然後你就會聞到勝利的氣味了。

TEST 小測驗

⭐ 1. 用英語說出下面有關運動的詞彙。

(a) 體操墊子　　(b) 平衡木　　(c) 鞍馬

(d) 網球場　　　(e) 網球球員　　(f) 球拍

(g) 球網　　　　(h) 網球　　　　(i) 網球鞋

⭐ 2. 用英語說出下面的運動項目。

(a) 田徑

(b) 武術

(c) 擊劍

(d) 溜冰

⭐ 3. 用英語說出下面的句子。

(a) 我喜歡做體操。
I love ...

(b) 我比較喜歡緩步跑。
I prefer ...

(c) 我不喜歡踢足球。
I ... ... playing football.

(d) 我比較喜歡打高爾夫球。
I ... golf.

DICTIONARY 詞典

（英、粵、普發聲）

A

archery　　射箭運動

athlete　　運動員

B

backhand　　反手擊球

backstroke　　背泳

balance beam　　平衡木

banner　　橫額

basketball court　　籃球場

basketball stand　　籃球架

bathing cap　　游泳帽

bathrobe　　浴袍

breaststroke　　蛙泳

butterfly stroke　　蝶泳

C

canoeing　　獨木舟運動

captain　　隊長

cartwheel　　側手翻

champion　　冠軍

changing room　　更衣室

climbing pole

　　　訓練爬行的柱子

club　　俱樂部

counter attack　　反攻

crawl　　自由泳

cup　　獎盃

cycling　　單車運動

D

defender　　後衞

diving board　　跳水板

dribble　　運球

E

extra time　　加時賽

F

fans　　球迷

fencing　　劍擊

field hockey　　陸上曲棍球

figure-skating　　花式溜冰

flag　　旗子

flip-flops　　平底人字拖鞋

foil　　劍術用的劍

football pitch　　足球場

forehand　　正手擊球

foul　　犯規

free throw　　罰球（籃球）

G

game　　局

goal　　球門

goalkeeper　　守門員

golf　　高爾夫球

gym mat　　體操墊子

gymnastics　　體操

H

hairdryer

　　風筒（普：吹風機）

high jump　　跳高

high jump crossbar

　　跳高用的橫木

horse riding　　騎馬

hurdle race　　跨欄跑

I

ice hockey　　冰上曲棍球

ice skates　　溜冰鞋

ice-skating　　溜冰

J

jogging　　緩步跑

judo　　柔道

K

karate　　空手道

kick-off　　開球

knee pads　　護膝

L

lane　泳道

linesman　巡邊員

lob　高吊球

locker　儲物櫃

long jump　跳遠

M

martial arts　武術

match　比賽

mattress　褥墊

N

net　球網

O

opponent　對手

P

parallel bars　雙槓

pass　傳球

penalty kick　罰球（足球）

pirouette　腳尖旋轉

player　球員

push-ups

　　掌上壓（普：俯臥撐）

R

race　賽跑

racket　球拍

referee

　　裁判（籃球、足球等）

results　比賽結果

rider　騎士

rings　吊環

rollerblades　滾軸溜冰鞋

roller-skating　滾軸溜冰

rope　繩子

S

sailing　帆船運動

save　成功救球

score　分數

scoreboard　記分牌

serve　　發球

set　　盤

shoot hoops　　射籃

shot　　射球

shot-putting　　推鉛球

shower　　淋浴

slam-dunk

　　入樽（普：灌籃）

smash　　殺球（普：扣球）

somersault　　翻筋斗

speed skating　　競速溜冰

split　　劈腿

stadium　　運動場

starting block　　出發台

swimming costume

　　泳衣（普：游泳衣）

swimming goggles

　　泳鏡（普：游泳護目鏡）

swimming lesson　　游泳課

swimming trainer　　游泳教練

T

target　　箭靶

tennis court　　網球場

time out　　比賽暫停

towel　　毛巾

track and field　　田徑

trainers　　運動鞋

U

umpire

　　裁判（棒球、網球等）

uniform　　制服

V

vaulting horse　　鞍馬

volley　　截擊凌空球

volleyball　　排球

W

water sports　　水上運動

whistle　　哨子

wind surfing　　滑浪風帆

winner　　優勝者

wristbands　　護腕

看在一千塊莫澤雷勒乳酪的份上，你學得開心嗎？很開心，對不對？好極了！跟你一起跳舞唱歌我也很開心！我等着你下次繼續跟班哲文和潘朵拉一起玩一起學英語呀。現在要說再見了，當然是用英語說啦！

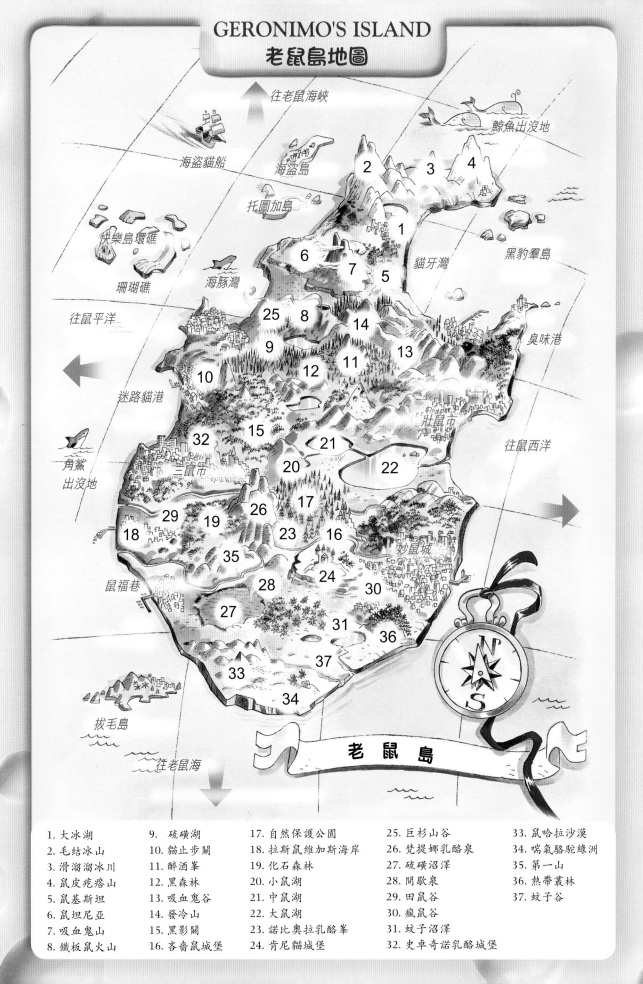

GERONIMO'S ISLAND
老鼠島地圖

往老鼠海峽

鯨魚出沒地

海盜貓船

海盜島

托圖加島

2　　3　　4

1

快樂島環礁

6

貓牙灣

黑豹羣島

珊瑚礁　　海豚灣

7　　5

臭味港

往鼠平洋

25　8

14

9

13

11

12

10

壯鼠市

15

32　　21

往鼠西洋

迷路貓港

二鼠市

20

22

角鯊
出沒地

17

29　19

26

23　16

妙鼠城

18

35

27

28　24

30

鼠福巷

31

33

37　36

34

拔毛島

往老鼠海

老 鼠 島

1. 大冰湖
2. 毛結冰山
3. 滑溜溜冰川
4. 鼠皮疙瘩山
5. 鼠基斯坦
6. 鼠坦尼亞
7. 吸血鬼山
8. 鐵板鼠火山

9. 硫磺湖
10. 貓止步關
11. 醉酒峯
12. 黑森林
13. 吸血鬼谷
14. 發冷山
15. 黑影關
16. 客魯鼠城堡

17. 自然保護公園
18. 拉斯鼠維加斯海岸
19. 化石森林
20. 小鼠湖
21. 中鼠湖
22. 大鼠湖
23. 諾比奧拉乳酪峯
24. 肯尼貓城堡

25. 巨杉山谷
26. 梵提娜乳酪泉
27. 硫磺沼澤
28. 間歇泉
29. 田鼠谷
30. 瘋鼠谷
31. 蚊子沼澤
32. 史卓奇諾乳酪城堡

33. 鼠哈拉沙漠
34. 喘氣駱駝綠洲
35. 第一山
36. 熱帶叢林
37. 蚊子谷

Geronimo Stilton

EXERCISE BOOK

練習冊

想知道自己對 LET'S KEEP FIT! 掌握了多少，
趕快打開後面的練習完成它吧！

ENGLISH!

6 **LET'S KEEP FIT!** 一起來健身！

I LOVE EXERCISING
我愛做運動

⭐ 從下面選出適當的英文詞彙，填在圖畫旁的橫線上。

> ribbon　　high jump　crossbar　　rings
> vaulting horse　　gym mat　　balance beam　　rope

1. _____

2. _____

3. _____

4. _____

5. _____

6. _____

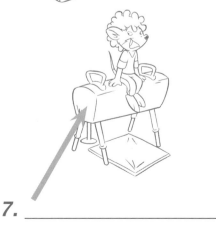

7. _____

A FOOTBALL MATCH
足球比賽

⭐ 根據圖意，從下面選出適當的動詞，填在橫線上。

has fouled	has to take	wins	has scored

1. Benjamin _____ a goal.

2. A player from the rival team _____ .

3. Rarin _____ the penalty kick!

4. Benjamin's team _____ the match 1-0.

A TENNIS MATCH 網球比賽

⭐ 你知道下面關於網球的英文詞彙的意思嗎？把相配的中英文詞彙用線連起來。

1. tennis court •   • 網球

2. umpire •   • 球網

3. tennis player •   • 網球場

4. wristbands •   • 球拍

5. net •   • 裁判

6. racket •   • 護腕

7. tennis shoes •   • 網球鞋

8. tennis ball •   • 網球球員

AT THE SWIMMING POOL
在游泳池

⭐ 從下面選出適當的英文詞彙，填在圖畫旁的橫線上。

bathing cap   swimming goggles   diving board
towel   starting block   swimming costume

1. _____

2. _____

3. _____

4. _____

5. _____

6. _____

PLAYING FOOTBALL 踢足球

⭐ 根據下面的圖畫，圈出正確的英文詞彙。

1.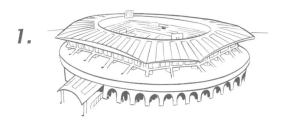

tennis court	stadium

2.

kick-off	serve

3.

fans	trainers

4.

football player	referee

5.

bathrobe	uniform

A BASKETBALL MATCH
籃球比賽

⭐ 根據下面圖畫的意思，把每題中的詞彙重新排列，使它成為意思完整的句子。

1.

Sakura / very / well. / dribbles

_____

_____

2.

Liza! / Excellent / shot,

_____

_____

3.

points / scores / two / with a slam-dunk. / Mohamed

_____

_____

4.

team / wins / the match. / Milenko's

_____

_____

HOORAY FOR SPORTS!
運動萬歲！

★ 看看下面的圖畫，然後選出代表正確答案的英文字母填在 □ 內。

A. high jump   B. karate   C. cycling
D. horse riding   E. ice-skating   F. sailing
G. archery   H. golf   I. roller-skating

1.  □

2.  □

3.  □

4. 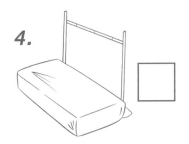 □

5.  □

6. 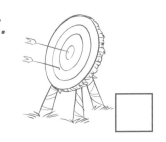 □

7. 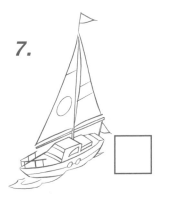 □

8. 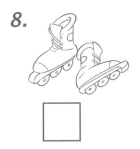 □

9.  □

ANSWERS 答案

TEST　小測驗

1. (a) gym mat　　(b) balance beam　　(c) vaulting horse　　(d) tennis court　　(e) tennis player
   (f) racket　　(g) net　　(h) tennis ball　　(i) tennis shoes
2. (a) track and field　　(b) martial arts　　(c) fencing　　(d) ice-skating
3. (a) I love gymnastics.　　(b) I prefer jogging.
   (c) I don't like playing football.　　(d) I prefer golf.

EXERCISE BOOK　練習冊

P.1
1. gym mat　　2. ribbon　　3. balance beam　　4. high jump crossbar
5. rope　　6. rings　　7. vaulting horse

P.2
1. has scored　　2. has fouled　　3. has to take　　4. wins

P.3
1. tennis court　網球場　　2. umpire　裁判　　3. tennis player　網球球員
4. wristbands　護腕　　5. net　球網　　6. racket　球拍
7. tennis shoes　網球鞋　　8. tennis ball　網球

P.4
1. starting block　　2. diving board　　3. swimming goggles
4. bathing cap　　5. swimming costume　　6. towel

P.5
1. stadium　　2. kick-off　　3. fans　　4. referee　　5. uniform

P.6
1. Sakura dribbles very well.　　2. Excellent shot, Liza!
3. Mohamed scores two points with a slam-dunk.　　4. Milenko's team wins the match.

P.7
1. H　　2. B　　3. D　　4. A　　5. C　　6. G　　7. F　　8. I　　9. E